Bubble
& Squeak

For James, with love - CV

For Clara, with love - JM

ORCHARD BOOKS
338 Euston Road, London NW1 3BH
Orchard Books Australia
Level 17/207 Kent Street, Sydney, NSW 2000
First published in 2013 by Orchard Books
ISBN 978 1 40831 366 4
Text © James Mayhew 2013
Illustrations © Clara Vulliamy 2013

1 3 5 7 9 10 8 6 4 2
Printed in China
Orchard Books is a division of Hachette Children's Books,
an Hachette UK company.
www.hachette.co.uk

Bubble
& Squeak

James Mayhew * Clara Vulliamy

ORCHARD

Bubble was a star!

People came from far and wide to
Mr Magnifico's famous show, just to see
Bubble perform her daring act . . .

... The Pyramid of Peril!

Night after night, Bubble found herself far above the audience with only a bouquet of flowers to help her balance. How everyone clapped and cheered!

Bubble travelled to all sorts of places with
her carefully packed trunk . . .

. . . but she never stayed anywhere long
enough to make any friends.

Of course, it was fun travelling with Yo-Yo and Noodle,

and Boris the strongman . . .

. . . Umberto the human cannonball,

and the trapeze girls, Mitzi, Maisie and Mo.

But they always seemed so busy and Bubble felt she just didn't quite fit in.

Every night, after the applause ended and the audience went home, Bubble returned to her carriage by herself. She was very lonely.

Then, one night . . .

Squeak!

Along came a little mouse, looking for
somewhere warm and dry.

He thought this looked like just the right sort of place.

He followed the sound of music
and the bright lights . . .

and, oh! What a sight!

He watched Bubble's performance with
shining eyes and his heart skipped a beat.
It was the most wonderful thing he had ever seen.

Every night, he watched Bubble from afar, with a sigh.

The little mouse longed
to tell her how much
he admired her,
but he was far too shy.

Bon Bons

And so he hid himself away . . .

And when the show moved on to another town,

the little mouse went too.

But then one day, Mr Magnifico was horrified
to discover his cheese was being nibbled.
He knew that meant one thing -

a mouse!

"Elephants don't like mice!"
he said to the troupe.
"We must catch him
before Bubble finds out."

And so the search began . . .

They all
looked
high . . .

. . . and low.

But they couldn't find the mouse anywhere.

Until one night . . .

"Gotcha!"

roared Mr Magnifico.
"Now out you go!"

He chased the little mouse outside.
"And stay away from my elephant!" he added.
"Elephants don't like mice."

The little mouse stood in the rain
and tried not to cry.

And then, slowly, he went on his way.

Just then, he heard the audience gasp!
Something was wrong . . . He started running back
and saw that Bubble had forgotten her flowers!
How would she balance without them?

How would she survive

The Pyramid of Peril?

He knew at once
that she was in
mortal danger!

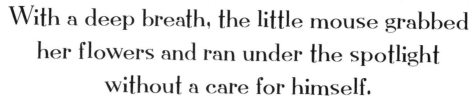

With a deep breath, the little mouse grabbed
her flowers and ran under the spotlight
without a care for himself.
The audience gasped.
"CATCH HIM!"
fumed Mr Magnifico.

But the mouse was too quick and too brave.

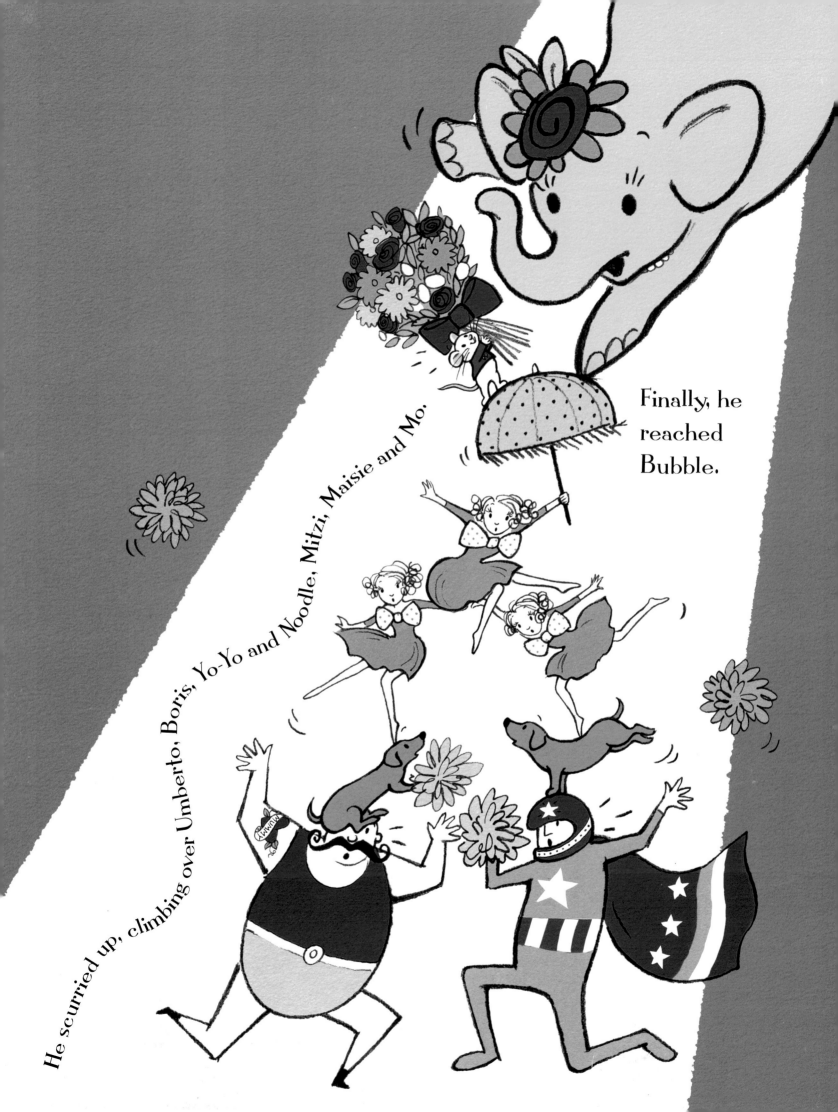

Finally, he reached Bubble.

He scurried up, climbing over Umberto, Boris, Yo-Yo and Noodle, Mitzi, Maisie and Mo.

She was safe at last.
"Oh bravo . . . how brave!"
said Bubble, too grateful to be scared.
"Squeak!" blushed the mouse.
The crowd cheered. They thought it was
the most marvellous act they had seen.
But it was Mr Magnifico who cheered the loudest.

"Your performance was wonderful," whispered the little mouse.
"I couldn't have done it without you," smiled Bubble.
"I've wanted to meet you for so long . . . " said the mouse.
"And I longed for a little friend . . . " said Bubble.

They talked and talked
into the night . . .

until they realised
they weren't shy or
lonely anymore.

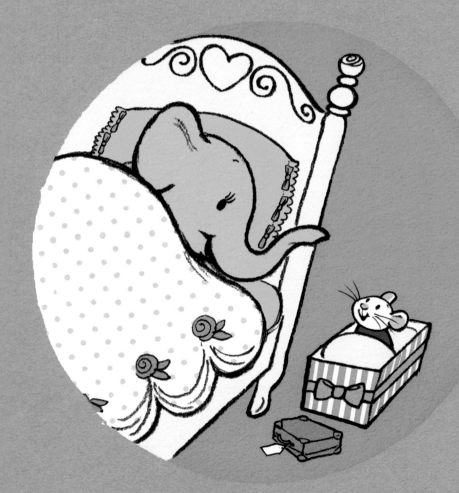

They were
happy!

"Do you think you might, perhaps, stay a while?"
asked Bubble. "We make a good team!"

And so Mr Magnifico asked the mouse to join the show.
"I'll give you all the cheese you could wish for.
But there's just one thing . . . you need a name.
Any ideas?"